Billy's Birthday Card

by Linda Wills
illustrated by Lance Ross

Harcourt
SCHOOL PUBLISHERS

Printed in the United Stattes of America

ISBN 10: 0-15-351355-1
ISBN 13: 978-0-15-351355-8

Ordering Options
ISBN 10: 0-15-351211-3 (Grade 1 Advanced Collection)
ISBN 13: 978-0-15-351211-7 (Grade 1 Advanced Collection)
ISBN 10: 0-15-358041-0 (package of 5)
ISBN 13: 978-0-15-358041-3 (package of 5)

2 3 4 5 6 7 8 9 10   179   15 14 13 12 11 10 09 08 07

Here I am, on the mat in Billy's house. I am a bright blue birthday card. I was sent by Billy's dad. He is away for his job. He was able to go to a card shop to get me.

Billy's dad put a stamp on me, and he took me to the mailbox. Then I was put in a bag in a mail truck. I traveled to the mail center to be sorted.

At the mail center, all the mail was poured out of the bag. All of a sudden, I was in a great big machine. The machine went around and around, and all the small mail stayed with me.

Then a machine turned me around so that my stamp was face up. The machine printed a mark on me.

A sorting machine sorted me into the right pile for my address. I went to the airport and onto a plane. The plane went into the sky. It was flying to Billy's city!

The plane landed. Then I was on my way to the mail center where Billy lives.

At the mail center, the mail was sorted into piles. One of the people at the mail center picked up my pile. She read Billy's address. Then she put me and some other mail in her mail bag.

She carried me up North Road in the mail bag. I was getting very excited! I was almost at Billy's house!

She carried me to the house. "Clatter!" went the mail slot at Billy's house. I fell onto the mat.

Now I hear Billy coming with his mom. They will pick up the mail. Billy will like me. He will get a great surprise!